S0-ARM-642

THE LONG ———

Awakening

Thanks

Russell B. Crites

— **Written by Russell B. Crites** —

ISBN: 978-1-300-85299-5

© 2013 by Russell B. Crites
Text © 2013 by Russell B. Crites

Cover design and layout by Eric Hanson, Solus Designs, LLC.

All rights reserved. This book may not be reproduced in whole
or in part by any means (with the exception of short quotes
for the purpose of review) without the permission of the publisher.

For more information, write Russell B. Crites,
P.O. Box 144, Gildford, MT 59525.

Created, produced, and designed in the United States.
Printed in the United States.

To the memory of my folks:
Bill and Pat I think I learned your lessons well. Thank you.

To my family:
Mary Pat, Lance, Nikki, Rhett, and Casey. If not for your love, support, and encouragement this life long dream would have never happened. Thank you from the bottom of my heart.

CONTENTS

CHAPTER ONE

IT WAS A TYPICAL HOMESTEADER SHACK except there were probably ones a lot cleaner. In fact probably all were a lot cleaner for this one belonged to Ray Frost, bachelor, drunk and sometimes farmer/rancher. When he wasn't roaring drunk and gone for days on end, he damn sure didn't care about the job of housecleaning. Well the truth of the matter was he was either drunk, hung over, sick or all three, most of the time.

If he did get any work done on the 320 acre plot of land in northern Montana it was by accident. He had come west to make his fortune he told people in Dayton, 15 miles to the south, but actually he was running away from his problems in Kansas. No one knew anything about his past except some of his drunken cronies in the pool hall in Dayton, but by the next morning they had forgotten his troubles in their own gray fog. Ray himself usually forgot that he had said anything in the haze of the morning after.

Montana in 1926 was a hard place to survive as the land was bleak and unforgiving. Most of the men like Ray fit right in, they were hard and intolerant especially to themselves.

Montana had been advertised as the land of Milk and Honey by the Great Northern Railroad with its founder Jim Hill as the architect. The idea was to get the people of the east, Midwest, west and Europe to come to this wind swept barren land which fried you in the summer and froze your ass in the winter. All you had to do was put up a homesteader shack and prove you could stick it out for a year. If you could survive the grasshoppers, the dust, the wind and the 30 below winter you were welcome to the 320 acres of gumbo or sandy land which usually blew away when you scratched the surface.

Hard land for hard people, they came in droves and left in droves. Some didn't last the first winter. The land was populated mostly by immigrants, either from the old countries of Germany, Norway, Sweden, or first generation Americans generally from the Midwest or, in Ray's case, Kansas. In fact, so many came from Kansas, they called certain areas around the Hi-Line of Montana Kansas Valley. They named this area of northern Montana the Hi-Line because the railroad rose up higher toward the Rocky Mountains in the west from Bull Hook Bottoms.

This was a new start for Ray when he came 15 years ago. All full of hope and running as fast as he could from his drinking problems, he came to make his fortune. What brought him and many others was the land. Land had a terrific pull for these people. To own land was the carrot in front of the donkey.

Only now, 15 years later, he was still drunk, still sick, still hungover, and the new start had certainly started looking like what he had left behind.

It was a morning in November when the land and the sky were both gray and Ray was awful sick. Searching for his bottle he knew he had the night before he was frantic to get a drink before the shaking started. "Damn I know I had that bottle somewhere," he said literally tearing the house to pieces looking. Real fear came when he found the empty whiskey bottle.

Nothing to do but to go saddle ol' Bouncer and ride the 15 miles to the pool hall in Dayton. Riding 15 miles sick and shaky wasn't going to be pleasant, but the alternative was worse. He couldn't believe he had come home without whiskey. "Dumb ass," he said to himself. On top of being sick and shaky he told himself he was the dumbest S.O.B. in the whole of northern Montana.

It's gonna be a helluva long ride to town.

CHAPTER TWO

OL' BOUNCER EARNED HIS NAME as Ray was jarred to death as he rode toward town. In between puking he allowed himself to look back. He hadn't always been this way. He hadn't known his real father; his mother had never talked about him.

He was raised on a farm in Kansas. His step-father was a German right from the old country. His mother was Welsh and English. They were both tee-totalers, but the old man had been a hell-raiser in his youth. He would always tell that strong drink lead to disaster. His mother had never had a drink as far as he knew.

They were church going people and attended a Lutheran Church in their small town.

He had no brothers or sisters so it was lonely growing up. His parents *were* there and he was there, nothing else. There wasn't much love; he was just another mouth to feed. They worked like hell just to survive. He couldn't remember any hugs or *I love yous* or much attention at all. He was expected to work as far back as he could remember. That's just the way it was.

He learned early on that you didn't cross the old man as he had an explosive temper. The temper would appear suddenly from out of the blue. If it did you needed to get out of the way, quickly. He would blow up like a stick of dynamite and would wreak havoc on anything that was near by. Later he would calm down and act as if nothing was the matter or there was no incident at all. Objects were broken, animals were kicked, bit or beaten and people too if they happened to be in the way.

His mother was just an onlooker with really no input or comment. She was just there. No one acted as if anything was ever out of the ordinary when the old man went off. Everyone learned to ignore and look the other way, clean up the mess and go on.

He had a great fear of his step-father which turned into hate. As he grew older his mother's indifference irritated him worse than his step-father's temper.

The only things that made it tolerable for him was the animals on the farm and he loved school. The country school he attended gave him a refuge from the work and the insanity of home. He loved reading and the old school had a fair library. He read all he could get his hands on. He read to escape the life he hated.

As soon as he was out of the 8th grade he lit out. Nothing could be worse than this he reasoned, but he was wrong.

CHAPTER THREE

RAY MADE HIS WAY TO KANSAS CITY and found work at a slaughter house.

A young man away from home, he soon found alcohol. At first he thought it solved his problems as reading had done in the past. Drinking gave him an escape and a refuge. Ray discovered, however, that the drinking soon became a worse problem than the ones he was trying to solve.

As he grew in years and size his alcohol troubles grew also. Fights, lost wages, blackouts and soon, trouble with the law. He sought out places and people who did the same things he did. Ray discovered card games and prostitutes.

The card games helped him on his way to his new life in Montana. As his gambling debts grew he knew he could never pay them so he was looking for a way out.

The kick in the pants toward Montana had come after a drunken fight. Ray had only a foggy recollection of the fight, but when he came out of the fog there was a fellow lying in a pool of blood not moving. Ray headed for Montana without knowing what ever happened to the man. This was just the final straw.

A new life, yes, but a wagon full of the past was pulled to Montana with him.

CHAPTER FOUR

THE LONG RIDE CONTINUED and the remembering stopped. He cursed himself for losing the old Model T in a card game. It would have been a much shorter ride. Then all was blank but the need for a drink.

Dayton, Montana in 1926 wasn't much to look at, a store, a few houses, a church and a pool hall. They were called pool halls not bars because this was prohibition, but they served the same purpose. Ray didn't pay any attention to the town because his mind was on a drink. A drink to kill the misery.

He tied up ol' Bouncer outside the pool hall and went for the door trying to keep his hands from shaking.

Whiskey was all he said to Red as he headed for the table in the corner. Red brought a bottle and a glass. Ray was grateful for the dark corner so he could hide his shaky hands and his spilling when he poured his drink.

Red Baker was used to Ray and his shakes. He'd seen him

worse, much worse, but he knew the routine. Ray needed about three stiff drinks to keep his hands from shaking and about a third of the quart of rot gut whiskey to start to get well. The process had been repeated many times the last four years since Red had come to Dayton.

The drink was hard enough to pour but really hard to keep down. The first couple was the trickiest. Shaking so badly most of it spilled on the table and when it hit bottom it was a chore to keep down. "How long was this gonna go on?" he asked himself. "I don't know how long I can stand this. Oh God help me."

This endless cycle had repeated itself for years. When he came north out of Kansas he had been 20 years old. Ray had come like many who with the promise of owning 320 acres of rich fertile land had come with high hope. This was the land that the Great Northern Railroad had advertised, a land of *Milk and Honey*. He had claimed his 320 acres and set up his homestead shack. He fell to work, there had been some real good years, but the last two or three, Ray and many others where just hanging on. Many had left and he had really thought he should too. What stopped him was he knew his troubles had come with him from Kansas and they would surely go with him again. Those that had left didn't feel as if they had a choice. The land was harsh, grasshoppers, drought, freezing wind and cold. Most of them went bankrupt. How Ray hung on with all of this and the constant drinking was hard to tell.

A few more drinks and the shakes would be gone

and maybe some of this mental anguish he lived with constantly. His companions where self-doubt and self incrimination for not being good enough or smart enough, whatever else was available to beat himself up with.

What he had learned at home was that he'd never amount to anything, that he was a burden, and no affection. These lessons were learned very well.

Lately, this seemingly endless cycle of drinking and getting sick was almost too much. The thoughts of suicide were always there. The old 32 special lever action Winchester rifle was always staring at him from the wall at home. He was afraid to be home with his thoughts and the old rifle.

Red broke into his daze by asking how long it had been since he had eaten. Ray just shook his head. Red made a comment that if you don't eat something we will get out the white gloves and throw dirt in your face by spring. Red turned and left Ray with his demons.

CHAPTER FIVE

WHEN OR HOW THE IDEA CAME TO HIM Ray couldn't remember. There it was just the same; there it sat in his mind. A mail-order bride would be the ticket. Ray may have seen it in a paper or maybe heard it from a fellow drunk, but anyway the idea stuck and it grew from there.

The thought pattern went something like this: "I'm damned lonely and since I'm lonely this is why I drink." The solution to all this is to get some gal from somewhere to move out here and instantly loneliness will be gone and presto no more drinking problem.

Made sense to Ray, but a drunk's mind is always looking for answers outside of oneself.

Out of this line of thinking hatched a plan. Ray would take out advertisements in four or five papers in the Midwest, south and the west for a helpmate, someone willing to move to this land of "Milk and Honey" and marry him. A tall order, he knew he would have to embellish it some to attract anyone at all. Bullshitting was not a problem for Ray Frost.

He spent weeks trying to figure out just what to say and how to write it. Finally he came up with the following: "Wanted: woman to help a rancher in northern Montana. Room and board and possibly matrimony. Write: Ray Frost, General Delivery, Dayton, Montana."

He sent five letters. Three to the south, one to the Midwest and one to the west. He was hopeful but apprehensive too. The old thoughts came to him about his being worthless and no good. When he drank he imagined no woman would ever answer any of the ads.

After weeks of waiting he decided to try a new approach, he wrote an ad and sent it to the Matrimonial News in the San Francisco paper.

The ad read:

Man 35 years old. 5 ft. 7 in. tall, 155 lbs.
Has good ranch home in Montana.
Looking for a woman for matrimony.

Good he thought, simple and straight to the point.
He sent it in and waited.

CHAPTER SIX

GERALDINE HARRISON WASN'T MUCH TO LOOK AT and she knew it. Her abusive father had made sure of that when he broke her nose when she was 14. Of course there was no trip to the doctor, so the nose healed rather crooked and to the side. Not that it made that much difference in her looks, but it was just one more thing.

She was raised in a very small town in eastern Washington State and had made it thru the sixth grade. She was expected to work after that and help support two little brothers and three sisters. Her mom died when she was born and her half sibling's mother was a Umatilla Indian from the nearby reservation.

When Geraldine read the ad in the Matrimonial Paper that was a couple months old she thought nothing could be worse then getting beat and taking care of five little ones.

Her writing wasn't the best but she managed to send a

note to Ray.

> Sir,
> I am willing to come to Montana
> if you would send me train fare.
> I am 18 yrs. old and can keep house.
>
> Geraldine Harrison
> Lowden, Washington

She didn't include a picture as she wanted to make sure he sent the train fare.

CHAPTER SEVEN

RAY WAS BESIDE HIMSELF WITH EXCITEMENT when the letter came. He had been drunk for days and very desolate. He went through a bad case of the shakes and was very sick for about three days, but the promise of a new beginning made it worthwhile.

He composed a letter to Geraldine and sent the money for her train fare. Ray told himself he was going to stay sober as a judge, because this was his whole problem. He convinced himself he drank because of loneliness and this was about to be solved.

He set about to work on the old homestead shack to make it somewhat presentable. It had not had a good cleaning since about two years before. It was an enormous task.

It was February so you couldn't just air out the place as it was 20 to 25 below zero some mornings. So the cleaning went slowly and the stench of a two year period of drinking disappeared even slower.

The shack was a one room affair about 20' by 12' with a wood stove in the corner used for heat and cooking. There was a bed, table, a couple old chairs, a few boxes used as cupboards and a wash stand. There was a door and a window neither of which kept much of the heat in or the cold out. There was no insulation except if you counted the newspapers pasted on the wall and stuck in the cracks. The shack was better than some on the prairie, but nothing to write home about.

Some of his neighbors with wives had improved on their one room affairs and had two or more rooms. Other homesteaders down Cottonwood Crick had nothing more than a *Soddy*.

A *Soddy* was a house made out of prairie sod cut in a square and about three to four inches in depth. These squares were cut to various sizes depending on who was doing it. They were then piled one on top of the other for walls. The roof over the walls was made of whatever wood was available and then sometimes it was covered with sod.

On the bottom end of the scale was a dugout which was dug in a hillside and covered with wood by itself, or wood with sod for the roof.

The bathroom for these mansions was the outdoor privy. A little shack with a seat made out of boards, and then a circle was cut into the seat to form a hole. This was affectionately known as the throne. Fancy privies had two holes. This structure was over a hole dug into the ground of various depths which depended on who was doing the digging.

When it was 40 below zero and the wind was howling you used a covered bucket in the house fondly called the *slop bucket.*

There was water, of course, from the well if you where lucky enough to have one. If you had a well you had to pump the water into a trough for horses and cows or buckets for people. Then depending on the distance you where from the house you had to carry enough water for drinking, cooking, cleaning and bathing. Notice bathing came last. If you didn't have a well on your property you depended on your neighbor's well or went to the crick. The trip was longer then and the water you brought to the house was used very sparingly. In all cases the running water people talked about in the big cities took on a whole new meaning on the prairie. Most of it was walking water as it was pretty hard to run with bucket of water without spilling and you didn't make any more trips than necessary.

There was a good well on Ray's place. It was right next to the barn and about 200 yards from the house.

This was the ranch house Ray had advertised in the Matrimonial Papers. He hadn't lied he just didn't elaborate.

CHAPTER EIGHT

THE SOBERING UP WASN'T EASY and staying that way was hell on earth. He walked the floor, he cleaned, he planned, he walked the floor some more. He even brought out his old tattered Bible his ma had given him as a youngster. He read and read. Finally he came to the scripture that read, "I can do all things through Christ that strengthen me." Ray hung onto that like a drowning man.

After he sent the money he felt like a fool. She probably was going to take the money and spend it right there. She would have a good laugh on him for his stupidity. If she didn't do that she probably would get cold feet and leave the minute she saw him. Maybe she was especially ugly, fat, or crippled. His thoughts raced on and on.

He decided if all of the above weren't true maybe she wasn't right in some way and someone had written the letter for her. He didn't sleep a helluva lot since he had sent the money off. If he wasn't thinking about a drink his mind was racing to all kinds of possibilities about Geraldine.

After a week of this he decided if she did show up he at least better marry her to make things right. He had gone to enough church when he was younger so he knew the difference between right and wrong.

Ray decided he had better go to town and talk to Reverend Barton, the traveling preacher about a wedding. He needed to get out of the shack before he went stir crazy.

CHAPTER NINE

ANOTHER LETTER ARRIVED FROM GERALDINE. She had received the money and had bought her ticket. She was supposed to arrive the 1st of March, 1927. She asked if Ray would meet her at the station.

As she rode the passenger train and got closer and closer to the Hi-Line of Montana, Geraldine kept asking herself if she was crazy. She had set off in late winter to meet a man three states away and hardly knew anything about him. She stared out the window at the barren landscape and the closer she got a storm hit with a vengeance.

What a welcome Montana gave this 18 year old girl on the first day of March. It had snowed steadily for about 12 hours and the wind was blowing at least 30 miles an hour. As she stepped off the train with her one small bag onto the platform in Dayton, you couldn't see across the way to the hotel and General Store to the northwest.

There to welcome her was Ray, nearly twice her age and

nervous as hell. When they stepped into the warm Great Northern depot he finally had a chance to look at her. She did the same at him, only with her it was just a glance.

CHAPTER TEN

IT SURE WASN'T LOVE AT FIRST SIGHT. Two different thought processes were going on.

When Geraldine looked at him she was startled by how old he looked. He really wasn't bad looking, but he looked older than his 35 years. Gray had invaded the black hair and the face was care worn and wrinkled. The stark reality of the situation really hit her as she stood in the depot. She had come this many miles running away from an intolerable situation, but even that looked better than the unknown she faced now. She could hardly nod her head when Ray asked if she was hungry.

Ray was thinking, "My God she's young." His primary thought was, however, she sure wasn't much to look at with her broken nose and her unsmiling face.

Some of the uncomfortable feelings lifted as they made their way south across the tracks to the only eatery in Dayton.

Ma Beck ran the eatery with a smile and a good sense of

humor. Everyone who came in the door was greeted with, "Howdee, how ya doin today?" If you didn't know her before you felt like you did when you left. Her Oklahoma background was in her speech and her hospitality. She was the best cook in town and she knew it. She was a large woman who had a heart to match. When she spotted the young girl with Ray she made sure and tried to make her feel at home.

Geraldine was bone tired, frightened and hungry. When she ate she at least got rid of the hunger.

Ray tried to strike up a conversation to no end. He finally gave up and said "Let's get you a room for the night and we'll take off in the morning for home." He added kind of after the fact that he would bunk in the barn where the horse was.

She forced a smile and said, "I hope you don't freeze to death."

Ray shook his head, "Nice and warm where the stable boy sleeps. I'll just bunk in there."

They made their way across the street toward the east and good as his word Ray got her a room for the night above the pool hall that Red Baker ran.

Ray showed her to her room and where she could wash up down the hall. He then took her to the back door and pointed to the privy through the snow.

After Ray left she dropped onto the bed exhausted and burst into tears. Maybe tomorrow things would be better on the Hi-Line of Montana.

CHAPTER ELEVEN

BOTH HAD SLEPT IN SPURTS AND FITS. She from being so tired and exhausted, her sleep wasn't sound. Ray's sleep was interrupted by his thoughts racing from one thing to the other. The black of night always makes things look worse.

When morning finally came Geraldine busied herself trying to make herself look presentable. She thought she may as well stay it can't be worse than at home. Her next thought was I hope he doesn't send me back.

Ray was full of self doubt and wondering if she would stay at all. His mind raced on with she probably doesn't like me and on and on. His step-father's voice was always in the back of his head saying, "How dumb are you?"

By the time he knocked on the door of her room he had convinced himself that she was probably already gone.

It startled him when she answered the door in a barely audible voice she managed to get out, "Good Morning."

He was almost tongue tied but finally blurted out, "If you want to go back to Washington I'll understand."

Well there it was thought Geraldine, he's gonna send me packing. Out loud she said, "I'd like to stay if you'll have me, I didn't come all this way to turn around and go back."

Ray outdid himself and said, "Well young lady I'd sure like you to stay if you want."

Things got better on both sides right away when the air was cleared.

Ray told her that he had talked to the parson and if it would be agreeable they could get married in awhile, that is, if both of them still wanted to. Until that time he would sleep on the floor of the shack. She quietly agreed.

"Well let's go eat and then we will see if we can go for home."

CHAPTER TWELVE

THE BLIZZARD HAD LET UP IN THE NIGHT. The morning was cold and the sunshine was brilliant against the white background. Geraldine got her first look at Dayton, Montana. The clap-board buildings were not too plentiful, but she was used to small towns. Raised in one of these small places she knew how people loved to gossip. She was sure that news of her arrival had spread by now. She hoped she could find a friend in this little burg.

The 15 mile ride north to the *ranch* was something to remember. Ray had borrowed a sleigh and a horse besides ol' Bouncer, his saddle horse. They bundled up and having tied Bouncer behind they started off.

The scene was out of this world to Geraldine because as far as you could see on the endless prairie was a sea of white on white. Off to the west she could see some mountains but Ray called them *hills*. They sure looked like mountains to Geraldine. Every so often Ray would say,

"That is the Franklin place or that is the Edwards place or the Soldiers ranch." It all looked the same to an 18 year old girl who had never seen this much snow or this much empty space. She felt very small and insignificant the further north they went.

She finally said, "It's very barren looking."

Ray said, "You'll get used to it."

Geraldine didn't say anything but she figured she surely wouldn't get used to it.

CHAPTER THIRTEEN

THE *RANCH* WASN'T ANYTHING LIKE what she had imagined. The homestead shack was small and although Ray thought it was clean, Geraldine thought it was a pig sty. She didn't say anything, but set to work. She was glad to have something to do instead of sitting around waiting, wondering and worrying.

Ray muttered something about how hard he had worked to get the place shipshape, she didn't comment just kept cleaning.

He eventually said he had chores to do and she nodded gratefully.

The house was finally getting a little heat as the stove put out some nice warmth. She felt good enough to take off her old threadbare coat and maybe felt a little more at home.

Geraldine thought it isn't much but at least it will be clean and went back to work.

She found some food in the boxes used for cupboards and set about cooking. She enjoyed cooking and to some degree cleaning. She knew she wasn't much to look at but she was confident in her ability to cook and clean. She felt in her element now and busied herself so she didn't have to think. She worked hard and enjoyed herself, for a brief time she didn't dwell on how lonesome this barren country looked and that the nearest neighbor was a mile and a half away.

CHAPTER FOURTEEN

RAY WAS NOW SOBER FOR ABOUT a month and it was getting harder by the day. He so wanted to be sober, but the self doubt and fear were always sitting on the edge of his mind. When you didn't have rot-gut whiskey to kill the thoughts they were hard to live with. Always they whispered in his ear, you aren't good enough, you will mess something up and on and on.

Geraldine had been in his home for five days now and so far he'd kept his word about sleeping on the floor. He had fought his urges to crawl into bed with her, but without whiskey he was able to keep his word. He knew however it wouldn't be long with or without whiskey he would give in.

Knowing this on the sixth day he announced if she was willing they would make the trip to town and get hitched.

Geraldine was still afraid but more so of going back where she had come, so she agreed. She never said much and today was no exception. She merely nodded her head and said that would be fine.

CHAPTER FIFTEEN

MARRYING REQUIRED A TRIP to Bull Hook Bottoms 30 miles to the east of Dayton. It took a better part of the day to get to Dayton, they stayed overnight and rode the train to Bull Hook Bottoms the next day.

After obtaining the license at the Mountain County Courthouse they rounded up two witnesses and Reverend Barton married them.

They spent their wedding night in a boarding house in Bull Hook Bottoms run by an elderly Negro lady everyone called Ma Felton. She fixed a supper of stew and bread for them. She winked to them about making too much noise.

The wedding night wasn't too much to remember. There was some crying and disappointment for Geraldine's part. Ray's only comment was, "you'll get used to it." She thought to herself that she would get used to it the same way she would get used to the big lonely country she had come to.

The next day they rode the train back to Dayton. When Geraldine asked Ray if there was someone he wanted to let know about them getting married Ray said, "No, I haven't contacted my folks since I left Kansas. No sense to do it now." There was no honeymoon planned or talked about. They set out to begin their life as a married couple on the barren wasteland known as northern Montana. She hoped for spring as they rode north in silence.

CHAPTER SIXTEEN

MARCH TURNED INTO APRIL and then into May. Winter lingered on but spring came finally after a terrible struggle. Green grass amongst the blue/green sage brush along Cottonwood Crick appeared.

Geraldine was overjoyed. She felt like dancing. It had been a long winter for all concerned. No matter she had only been here three months, she was ready for spring.

She had cleaned and cleaned. Now she could go outside or open the doors and windows and let the smell of winter out and the intoxicating smell of spring in the North Country come in.

Geraldine had finally met a friend, their nearest neighbor to the southeast. Lucille Soldier was a cheery, bright, smiling girl of 23. She was only a mile and a half away and the two took to each other like sisters.

Lucy told her some wonderful gossip to keep Geraldine going, but also passed on some disturbing news, that

Ray had just quit drinking before Geraldine had come to Montana. Geraldine was more than a little worried. She had seen what drink can do to a person. One more worry she thought.

When Geraldine had missed a couple of months of her period, she confided in Lucy first about the possibility of pregnancy. Lucy was overjoyed as she had two kids of her own. She was a source of a ton of information about what to expect.

Geraldine put off telling Ray for about another week or so. When she worked up the courage to tell him he danced a little jig for her.

"If I was a drinking man I'd go to town and celebrate," yelled Ray, as he danced around the small homestead shack. He grabbed her and said he loved her. He was happy as hell.

Geraldine was startled as this was the first time he'd said he loved her. As usual she didn't say much, just nodded her head. She had gotten used to Ray who could carry on a conversation with himself for hours. He more or less talked to her, but it was more of a rambling dissertation on a lot of subjects and life in general. It wasn't designed for a response. All she had to do was to shake her head yes or no once in awhile and he would really go on for hours.

CHAPTER SEVENTEEN

RAY WAS BUSY AS COULD BE. His small ranch/farm had been sorely neglected the last few years of his drinking. He set about to right that and worked as if he was there was no tomorrow.

Geraldine loved the spring which had now turned into early summer as June arrived. She had the habit of opening the window and leaving the door and the old screen door open. She loved the fresh air. She had gone to the well which was about 200 yards from the house, and was returning with two buckets of water, when she suddenly dropped the buckets to the sound and sight of a big old prairie rattle snake. He was coiled and rattled out his warning. She screamed and ran for Ray who was working in the field with a single bottom plow and a team of horses.

He heard her before he saw her. He thought maybe the house was on fire. Then he heard, "Snake!! Snake!!"

He took her by the hand and ran to the barn where he got a shovel. It didn't take Ray long to chop the snake's head off and cut the rattles off with his jack knife as a souvenir.

Ray tried to give Geraldine his trophy, but all she could do was to shake her head. He said, "If you are gonna live out her you will have to get used to snakes."

Geraldine added that to the list of things she darn sure wasn't gonna get used to. She didn't leave the screen door open after that morning. All she could think about was that snake ending up in her house.

CHAPTER EIGHTEEN

BOTH RAY AND GERALDINE were very excited. Today was the 4th of July, 1927 and they were headed to Dayton for the town's celebration and rodeo. Big Henry Sims along with Mary Gifford from Little Sage were supposed to ride in the rodeo. A lot of local talent would be riding too. There was a promise of a firework display in the evening.

Ray, although excited, was more than a little nervous. It had been about four months since he had taken a drink and he knew that here in Dayton on the 4th of July all his friends would be drinking. Even though this was prohibition there would be moonshine whiskey all around and homemade beer. Geraldine didn't have a clue about the war going on inside of Ray's mind. She was just happy to be going to town. Their neighbors, Frank and Lucy Soldier, would be there and they would all have a picnic lunch together.

The rodeo grounds in Dayton where west of town and

consisted of a large enclosure and holding pens, chutes and gates for the animals. The human accommodations were rough with just a few bleachers, mostly you had to stand by the fence.

Big Harry Sims didn't disappoint as he rode a rough bronc named Graveyard. Mary Gifford also rode, she had been all over the good ol' USA and was probably the most famous woman bronc rider.

The day went well in spite of all of Ray's worrying. He kept close to Geraldine, Frank and Lucy. He turned down several invitations for a snort or two.

He actually had fun watching Geraldine's face at the Rodeo seeing the bronc busting and the steer wrestling. She was in total amazement, she even managed a couple of smiles.

The best event of the day was the wild cow milking contest. This is where a cow, fresh from the open range and never been milked before, is roped by one or two cowboys then the third cowboy tries to get a pint of milk from the unwilling participant. Geraldine actually laughed so hard she nearly doubled over when one cowboy got manure in his face for his trouble and was rudely kicked in the backside.

CHAPTER NINETEEN

SUMMER IS ALWAYS BUSY in the North Country. Winter is long and hard, spring lingers on, but summer is a whirlwind of activity. All the pent up energy stored up in winter, plus the shortness of the summer all add up to a blur of activity.

Ray kept extremely busy one because it was summer, two because everything had been neglected for so long. When he was busy he didn't have to think about the drink. He had a purpose and a goal, but always in the background lurking, biding its time, waiting patiently for the opportunity, was the drink.

Geraldine was busy too, but it didn't keep the loneliness away. Lucy was a mile and half away, she was busy too. Geraldine had heard of people going crazy on the vast empty prairie and you could see why. It's hard to be by yourself day after day. Geraldine had heard Lucy and Frank talk about a woman out south of Dayton hanging a dress on the clothes line and talking to it for company. Geraldine wasn't at that point but she sure was lonely.

The monotony was broken up one day when Ray came home and announced that the Linderman's, who lived about four miles to the northeast, had invited them to a barn dance on Saturday night.

Geraldine was ecstatic. She was finally going to meet some people. This was something to look forward to. Saturday night couldn't come fast enough.

CHAPTER TWENTY

GERALDINE PREPARED SOME FOOD and took some of their supply of coffee to the doings as they called it in the North Country.

She was very excited when they hitched the team up and set off on Saturday afternoon.

As they topped the hill above the Linderman's homestead they saw quite a number of wagons, buggies, Model T's and saddle horses around the two room shack. The shack was a little bigger than most as two homestead shacks had been put together to make one.

Geraldine soon found out the term barn dance didn't necessarily mean barn. All the furniture was taken out of the house and soon the sound of an old fiddle, a mandolin and a harmonica, called a *Jew's harp*, was heard.

A table was set up outside consisting of two saw horses and three or four planks stretched across to make the table. The food was all placed on the table and the eating began.

Geraldine was introduced to all kinds of folks. She was painfully shy, but it was hard not to be drawn into this friendly crowd. Everyone talked and laughed, what a wonderful interlude from the dullness of their lives.

The dancing began in the house and Geraldine was invited inside and soon was dancing. She had learned at an early age so it was just fun to move to the sawing of the fiddle and the strumming of the old mandolin. Someone played the harmonica for a few of the tunes and there was always someone trying to sing. Some sang better than others, but it didn't matter as it was all in good fun.

The kerosene lamps were trimmed and lit and the dancing continued late into the night.

Sometime later as she was in the house dancing and visiting and happily clapping her hands to the music Geraldine looked around and couldn't see Ray anywhere in the house. She just thought he had stepped out to the outdoor privy or was visiting with some of the older folks sitting around outside smoking.

After about another 15 minutes she decided she would step outside and see where Ray was. It didn't take much hunting to find him in a group of seven or eight men sitting in kind of a semi circle around a small campfire. The men were laughing and telling stories, smoking hand rolled cigarettes and pipes. But the thing that immediately caught Geraldine's eye was that they where passing around a jug of moonshine.

CHAPTER TWENTY-ONE

GERALDINE COULD SEE THAT RAY was drinking, but in spite of all she had heard from Lucy and others she wasn't too concerned. Ray was kind and thoughtful. She thought maybe he could do a little drinking now and then. "What could it hurt?" She said this to herself on the inside but she was feeling uneasy as she tried to convince herself.

She went through the motions of being unconcerned so she turned and went back inside the shack where the dancing and the playing continued.

Ray's justification for the drink was, "I've been sober for a few months and a little won't hurt." All the misery and pain he had suffered just left his mind and was replaced by anybody can have a drink, it won't hurt.

One drink lead to another, then oh well we may as well have one more. Ray was pretty stewed by the time Geraldine came out again to check on him. He had undergone a drastic change from her husband to another person she hardly recognized. He was swearing profusely and slurring his words. He was loud and boisterous right on the verge of combativeness.

Geraldine quietly suggested to him maybe they should head on home. Ray promptly turned and said, "Don't tell me what to do woman. I'm the boss around here and we'll go when I'm damn good and ready."

Later, much later, Ray lay passed out near the campfire. Geraldine was really upset and embarrassed. Almost everyone there had seen Ray perform or saw him passed out as they left. Guy Linderman helped her hitch the team and load Ray into the wagon on a bed of canvas sacks.

Geraldine headed for home in the dark hoping she could find her way. She also hoped the horses had a good sense of where home was since there was no moon to help her on her way. She prayed the horses wouldn't shy from some stupid jack rabbit jumping up in their path.

They reached home about 3 A.M. and Geraldine, not knowing what else to do, left the horses hitched to the wagon. She tied them to the hitching post outside the barn. She went to the house and came back with an old quilt and covered Ray still in the back of the wagon. She left him to sleep it off.

So much for "one drink wouldn't hurt."

CHAPTER TWENTY-TWO

MORNING WAS PAINFUL FOR RAY. He woke groggily from the bright sunshine. His mouth tasted like dried sawdust. It felt as if a little man was trying to kick out the inside of his head with hob-nailed boots. His eyes were bleary and he couldn't focus. He had extreme thirst and was really disgusted as he realized he had wet himself.

He literally crawled out of the wagon and made his way to the horse trough where he washed his face and soaked his head in the cool water. He couldn't look at his own reflection in the water as disgusted as he was. Finally he pumped some water and took some drinks. Immediately he threw the water back up and again ended up on his hands and knees puking. When there was nothing left but bile in his throat he stumbled to his feet and made his way back to the team still hitched to the post. He succeeded in getting the harness off and let them go into the corral. They were thirsty too, but not for the same reason as Ray.

He threw them a little hay and stopped to rest.

I could sure use a drink to get well Ray thought, but he knew no whiskey was on the place, so a shaky sick day was ahead.

He washed himself again in the horse trough and tried to stop shaking without much success. He then ran to the outdoor privy, and was grateful that there were two holes, one to puke in and one to get rid of the diarrhea. After a half hour session in the privy he made his way back to horse trough, then lay down in the shade by the barn.

He lay there for about a half and hour and then made his way sheepishly to the house.

CHAPTER TWENTY-THREE

NOT A WHOLE LOT OF ANYTHING was said throughout the day. Both sides were pretty quiet. One out of fear and one out of guilt and shame.

The fearful one wondered all day about what was coming next. The guilty shameful Ray just tried to survive the day.

Toward evening the sickness and the shakes kind of subsided and he was able to keep his supper down.

After supper as they sat at the table he looked Geraldine in the eye and said rather meekly, "Guess I should stay away from that drinking."

Geraldine didn't know what to say so she said nothing.

Ray said, " I promise you I will stay sober for you and our child." Ray meant every word and Geraldine believed him.

That night when they went to bed Geraldine told him she loved him and they both shed a few tears.

All was well for now.

CHAPTER TWENTY-FOUR

SUMMER MADE ITS WAY TO FALL and the leaves on the cottonwood trees along the crick turned gold and yellow. The nights were cold and there was frost on everything in the mornings.

Geraldine was getting more and more uncomfortable with the pregnancy. Ray had been sober since the barn dance. He had been good to his word.

Harvest had come and gone with its whirlwind of activity and the neighbors joined together to help each other with the work that needed to be done. The wheat crop had been the best Ray had raised in quite a few years.

Life had settled into a routine and Geraldine and Ray were comfortable with it and each other. Always lurking in the background of their minds was the drink or the threat of a drink.

They both chose to ignore it, but it didn't go away. It always was there.

Ray kept extremely busy and kept away from town and the gatherings of neighbors after work where they shared the bottle. He busied himself with work and tried not to think about anything but Geraldine and the baby that was coming.

Lately they had been traveling the six miles each way to the northwest to church on Sunday.

Brother Hal, the traveling minister, was there some Sundays and when he wasn't one of the deacons of the Lutheran Church of the Prairie read the Bible and gave a few thoughts on what was read.

Geraldine said she wanted her child to be brought up in the church, and Ray hoped the atmosphere would help him stay sober.

The highlight of every Sunday morning was watching Missus Olga Helgeson from down the road toward Silverstone. She had a no-good husband who didn't work. His whole purpose in life was to gamble and drink. He had presented Olga with six boys from 4 to 14 and one daughter who was the baby. Of course old Ole didn't come to church with Olga.

She and her baby daughter sat in the back of the church, but she placed all six boys in the front pew hoping that this would be a deterrent to their misbehavior. No such luck as about two minutes into the service two of the six would start a fight. It was always entertaining to watch a 200 plus pound woman scurry from the back of the church to the front and pull the ears of the offenders.

There was a pool every Sunday as to how many times this large woman would make a trip from the back to the front of the church. Winner would collect after church.

So much for listening to the message.

CHAPTER TWENTY-FIVE

FALL LINGERED THRU OCTOBER and Geraldine learned this beautiful time of year when the days were sunny and warm was called Indian summer. The nights were cold and frost usually was present in the mornings, but the days they more than made up for the cold nights.

Always, however, winter follows the fall and the time for their baby was coming soon.

Geraldine prayed that everything would be alright and the baby wouldn't come in the middle of a big blizzard. She at least wanted to be able to go to town or to Northby a little town west of Dayton where there was a small hospital.

Geraldine was about to learn babies come when they want to not when they are expected.

CHAPTER TWENTY-SIX

GERALDINE KNEW IT WAS TIME, so Ray went to get Lucy. There was not time to go to town. Geraldine knew they wouldn't make it.

When Lucy came Geraldine was already in intense labor. The labor went on for half a day with a lot of pushing and pain. Finally about 6 P.M. on the 3rd of December 1927 baby Marjory Lorene Frost was born. Mother and child were exhausted, but happy. Not any happier than Ray who had been around a lot of births on the farm but never anything this emotional for him. He was beside himself with joy. This finally made him feel his life had meaning and purpose. That little one in his wife's arms was a part of him. This was his extension into the future. He was overwhelmed. He made for the barn with an excuse to feed the livestock. He didn't want anyone to see him cry. Crying in northern Montana for a man was a sin and a weakness.

In the cover of the old barn he was safe to cry for joy.

CHAPTER TWENTY-SEVEN

THAT WINTER WAS MILD in comparison to the previous one. Geraldine started to have some affection for the land and the beautiful mountains to the west. They were called the Sweet Grass Hills. The mountains were striking on the days they looked a sapphire blue against the orangey red of the sky. The sight of them took her breath away with their beauty. Geraldine and Ray grew closer and they both marveled at the little one they had brought into the world. She was the center of attention and made their otherwise dreary world light up.

She literally did light up the room with her smile and her laughter. Every day was a joy for her parents to watch her grow and learn.

Several times that winter Geraldine tried to get Ray to write his folks to let them know about their marriage and Marjory. He said he'd think about it. In the end he couldn't bring himself to do it. He didn't feel close at all to his folks.

Besides, he was carrying a lot of guilt for not being in contact with them all those years.

Winter was open with some snow and cold, but always the warm wind from the southwest came and melted the snow. This warm wind in the winter Geraldine learned was called a Chinook, an Indian word which means *snow eater.*

March came in like a lamb and sure enough went out like a lion. A terrible blizzard hit around the 29th of March and lasted for days.

CHAPTER TWENTY-EIGHT

WHEN THE BLIZZARD QUIT and the drifts started to melt the North Country was a sea of mud and dirty running water.

Cottonwood Crick ran out of its banks and travel was pretty much limited to trips to the barn and back. Even a trip to the neighbors was out of the question.

Geraldine understood why this kind of loneliness and isolation would push a person over the edge of sanity if it went on and on.

There were always stories of someone going insane on the prairie. There were stories of mothers murdering their children, women talking to imaginary people. If you couldn't deal with the hardships and the isolation you simply cracked or packed your belongings and left. Many did in those years. Farm houses were abandoned and homesteads left. When a house was abandoned people just took what was necessary. The house then became fair game for the young boys in the area to come in and see what was still available. Some called the empty houses the *country store*. Some of the houses had everything left except the prior occupants clothes. There were guns, dishes and furniture gathering dust from the wind. There was always the west wind and the dust.

Geraldine coped fairly well most of the time because of her love for Marjory and her continuing care for Ray.

The isolation was very hard at times and by spring Ray and Geraldine both had cabin fever and felt a little stir crazy.

Sometime in the past winter Ray had mentioned going to the Stone Child reservation south east of Dayton to a real Indian pow wow.

This became the subject of a lot of winter conversations as Geraldine had never really been around Indians, the noble *Red Man*.

CHAPTER TWENTY-NINE

FINALLY THE WIND DRIED THE MUD so Ray and Geraldine could at least go to the neighbors. Spring fever was in the air and the activity during the daylight hours was almost non-stop.

Ray set to repairing fences and the barn. He got ready to seed a crop, and tilled the land. Both he and Geraldine were just grateful to get the hell out of the house into the fresh air.

Geraldine busied herself doing things outside as much as possible. She had Ray tear up a small patch of ground for a garden. With the help of Lucy she planted several small cottonwoods and some prairie flowers that were transplanted from the banks of the crick.

Geraldine kept an eye on Marjory and watched her steady progress toward crawling to walking. She was overjoyed with her no matter what. Raising a baby on the prairie was a chore, but Geraldine didn't mind at all.

Between cooking and cleaning there was always the wash. Diapers were made from old cotton cloth and the wash was done in an old tin tub with a wash board. Clothes were hung on a line. The lye soap left Geraldine's hands far from soft.

CHAPTER THIRTY

A TRIP TO STONE CHILD RESERVATION for a real Indian pow wow. This had Geraldine very excited. Ray had attended one before, but it certainly wasn't old hat.

They took the wagon and made the trip to Big Muddy the last town before the reservation. They slept in the wagon outside the livery stable under the stars.

The next morning, after breakfast at Big Muddy's only restaurant, they started out for the rez as all the locals called it.

When they arrived at the campsite for the pow wow Geraldine was alive with anticipation and a small amount of fear. Everywhere she looked she saw Indians, real honest to goodness Indians more than she had ever seen before all in one place.

She learned from Ray that a pow wow was a gathering of Indians usually from different places, to dance, sing and visit old friends and make new ones. They came to gamble too, playing the bone or stick game.

The costumes and regalia were something to take your breath away. There were buckskins and beads and feathers all around. Brightly colored costumes were the rule of the day.

Right after they got there the grand parade or entrance started. All the Indians in their costumes marched by. The participants were accompanied by singing and drum playing. It was an impressive sight, so different then anything Geraldine had ever seen.

The different dances started and Geraldine was amazed with the amount of endless energy the dancers seemed to have. The beating of the drums and rhythmic singing was a little eerie to Geraldine. Marjory was more than a little scared by some of the singing and began to cry. They moved away from the dancers and began to watch the gambling games.

Ray tried to explain that a lot was bet on each game. "In the old days," he said, "horses, buckskins, weapons and who knows what else was bet, now money was in the middle."

The players sat facing each other with 8 to 10 people on each team. Each had a leader on their side. The leader appeared to be reaching in a bag and bringing forth some bones. Then he tried to hide the bones in his hands. Some of the bones appeared to be marked and some were plain. The other side, or team, through their leader, tried to guess which hand certain bones were in. If they guessed right a stick went to the side that guessed right. It looked as if there were 10 sticks on each side and the object was to win all your opponents sticks by guessing where certain bones were.

This was all accompanied by the onlookers betting between themselves and constant singing and drumming.

Soon the singing didn't bother Marjory at all and she was sound asleep, not caring who won or lost.

CHAPTER THIRTY-ONE

THE TRIP HOME FROM THE *REZ* took a couple days and Geraldine sensed a real change in Ray. He was usually talkative and open, but now he seemed moody and edgy. She finally asked if she had done something and she got an abrupt response of "What the hell are you talking about?" She didn't ask anymore questions.

Inside of Ray a war was going on. He didn't really understand himself, but he was restless, grouchy and out of sorts. He told himself he should be happy after all he had a nice wife and a beautiful baby girl. It didn't matter something was still wrong and he couldn't put his finger on it.

When they got to Dayton Ray dropped Geraldine off at the store to get a few things and to visit mainly showing off Marjory to anyone who asked.

Ray made his way to the pool hall with the excuse to himself that he saw old man Wilson's Model T outside and needed to talk to him about a piece of machinery he had.

Pete Wilson was sitting at the end of the bar and obviously was about three sheets to the wind.

Ray sat down and before he could open his mouth Red had put a whiskey in front of him.

Ray didn't think about anything but picked up the drink and downed it. For a moment he thought, "What am I doing," but it was gone in an instant as the drink hit his stomach.

CHAPTER THIRTY-TWO

RAY LEFT THE POOL HALL SOON AFTER. Pete Wilson was in no shape to talk.

Geraldine almost immediately smelled the whiskey on Ray's breath, but said nothing. Although she was a little anxious she thought, "He isn't drunk and he wasn't gone very long so he'll be alright."

The trip out north was not too bad, but neither person spoke very much. Marjory was sleeping and Geraldine and Ray each were lost in their own thoughts.

Ray was congratulating himself with only having one drink and Geraldine was thinking how he was able to walk away from the pool hall. She had a vague feeling of apprehension but shook it off.

Summer was turning into fall and the crops were ripening. Soon the harvest would begin with a lot of work from daylight to dusk. Both people knew when Ray was busy he was safe.

CHAPTER THIRTY-THREE

FOR A GOOD MONTH RAY PATTED HIMSELF on the back for being so strong as to walk away from just one drink.

He needed to go to town on this Saturday as he needed some supplies and there was a break in harvest.

He made his way from the general store to the south side of the tracks to a kind of hardware store by the crick. He purchased a handle for a pitch fork he had broken and a few nails for the barn and some staples for fencing.

Ray thought, "Well, I'll just stop at the pool hall to see who's around."

He walked into the pool hall about one o'clock in the afternoon. The next time he looked at the clock it was seven in the evening. He had stopped for one drink, but that was six hours ago.

"Oh well," he thought, "I work hard I deserve to let a little steam off."

The pool hall was almost full tonight as some of the

harvest hands were in town and others were the regulars.

One of the men Ray was drinking with was Julius Albertsen who was a depot agent for the Great Northern Railway at Dayton. Julius was an old bachelor and spent most of his evenings drinking and playing cards.

About 9 o'clock Julius excused himself and said he had to go to the depot which was on the north side of the tracks almost directly across from the pool hall.

About a half an hour later Sam Moore, a farm hand and a barfly, hollered in the door of the pool hall that there was a dead man on the tracks.

Ray and some others burst out of the door to investigate.

The moon was full as they headed for the tracks. The first sight Ray had of anything was a man's hand lying between the rails, only a hand very white, lit up by the moonlight.

Ray was suddenly sober as he recognized the ring on the hand. "My God," he hollered, "its Julius."

The rest of poor Julius was found and brought to the depot platform and laid carefully on an old tarp someone had found. More than one man puked his rotgut whiskey up on the tracks with the grisly work. Ray was one of them.

Ray was more than a little shook up and decided it was time to ride Ol' Bouncer for home.

CHAPTER THIRTY-FOUR

GERALDINE WAS VERY WORRIED and hadn't really slept much at all. At about 5:30 A.M. she heard Ray close the barn door. She then pretended to sleep when he climbed into bed.

She could smell the whiskey and when Ray was snoring fitfully she broke down and cried. She was really scared.

When Ray awoke he told Geraldine about poor Julius. He related the whole grisly tale about Julius getting hit by a westbound train in front of his own depot. He neglected to tell her he had been drinking with him beforehand and made it sound as if the accident had happened much earlier in the evening. He told it like this was the reason he had stayed so long at the pool hall and drank so much because he was upset about poor Julius. Well so much for telling the truth. He didn't like to lie, but he rationalized that this would be easier on Geraldine and would justify his drinking to her and himself.

He had a slight case of the shakes that Sunday morning

and needless to say there was no six mile journey to the little white church to the northwest.

All Ray could think about that day was a drink. Guilt was his companion, but the desire for drink was back and occupied his thoughts. The obsession had returned.

CHAPTER THIRTY-FIVE

HARVEST WAS FINALLY OVER and another trip to town was in order. Ray had some bills to take care of and some supplies to get.

Geraldine and Marjory rode with him to Lucy's. She was going to visit for the day and let Marjory play with Lucy's kids.

Both people knew Ray was going to drink again. Geraldine just hoped against hope he would rise up and control his drinking. Ray just knew where he was headed to let off a little steam.

Ray paid a couple of bills and headed to the pool hall with the intention just to stay for a couple of hours and shoot the breeze with the boys.

At 9 o'clock at night Ray glanced at the clock, he promptly went back to his whiskey. Ray was deep in conversation with Molly Anderson, who was the town barfly. She wasn't much to look at when you were sober, but seemed to take on a different light when your belly was full of rot-gut whiskey.

Molly had slept with half the population of Dayton and was working on the other half. The boys called her *ol' mattress back.*

Sober Ray would have walked away the minute Molly came around but drinking he had other ideas.

They ended up in Molly's room at the Hotel Bar on the north side of the tracks near the General Store. The bed shook when a train went by and the pitcher on the bed stand tried to rattle off.

When Ray woke up at 5 A.M. Sunday morning he couldn't really figure out where he was for a few seconds. When he looked over at Molly snoring away on the other side of the bed he became physically sick. He barely made it down the hall to the shared washroom to puke his guts out. He puked and puked until there was nothing left but bile. His body trembled with the retching. Finally he was able to take the wash basin out of the room and go outside and throw the puke into the alley. He washed his head under the pump by the horse trough in back.

He slunk back inside to get his hat and shirt hoping against hope Molly wouldn't wake up or the gossipy Larson family who ran the Hotel Bar wouldn't see him.

He replaced the wash basin in the common bathroom and glanced at himself in the mirror. He hated who he saw and wanted to smash the reflection with his fist. The only reason he didn't hit what he hated was he didn't want to wake anyone up.

He grabbed his hat and shirt and made his escape. He went to the stable and got ol' Bouncer, leaving some money for his care. He started for home, sick, full of despair and not quite sober.

CHAPTER THIRTY-SIX

ON THE LONG RIDE HOME RAY WAS SICK AT HEART. He stopped often to puke adding to the feeling of despair. He made up a dozen stories then discarded them as he had discarded his sobriety.

He finally settled on the line of, "it's my business what I do and I'm the husband."

Geraldine saw him coming from a distance and not having slept most of the night was in part relieved to see him yet disgusted and broken hearted too.

It was a long Sunday for all concerned. Ray lay down and slept fitfully and Geraldine tried to busy herself with her chores. Marjory unaware of all the problems gurgled and talked gibberish.

Later in the day Geraldine decided the best approach was nothing at all so the silent treatment was on. Ray decided that was fine and out to the barn he retreated.

Both people chose to ignore each other and the situation. By ignoring it maybe they thought it would get better or go away. Neither was going to happen, and the sad thing was, deep down they both knew it.

CHAPTER THIRTY-SEVEN

IT WAS A BEAUTIFUL DAY IN THE MIDDLE OF SEPTEMBER. The sun was shining and it was very pleasant. Geraldine had gotten water from the well and heated it on the wood stove after breakfast. She had taken the old galvanized tin tub down and carefully checked the temperature of the water as she emptied the teakettles into the tub.

She added a little scented soap she had gotten in town last summer especially for Marjory's bath water.

She stripped Marjory down and having put the tub in the sunshine near the door with only the old screen door closing off the outside and the regular door open. She didn't think to latch the screen door.

Geraldine put Marjory in the tub and washed her. She had put a little wooden boat in the tub for her to play with. Geraldine let Marjory play in the two inches of water in the bottom of the tub and then busied herself with getting lunch ready.

She didn't hear the old screen door open and shut. The

old boar pig made his way inside by putting his nose in the loose fitting door and squeezing inside.

What she did hear finally was Marjory giggling and cooing.

When Geraldine turned she about had a heart attack. Marjory was laughing because the old boar was drinking the bath water at her feet and his nose or whiskers must have tickled Marjory's feet.

All Geraldine could see was a 5 ½ foot long 3 ½ foot tall boar hog with tusks at her daughters feet. Carefully, Geraldine picked up the iron skillet off the stove and padded silently to the tub.

With her left hand she grabbed Marjory and with her right she hit the boar as hard as she could with the skillet.

The boar squealed in pain and made for the screen door which he took off its hinges as he departed.

Geraldine was still shaking as Ray ran through the screen-less door frame.

When Geraldine managed to spit out how the monster boar had tried to eat Marjory in the tub they both suddenly stopped and looked at Marjory still naked and dripping wet from her bath. She was still smiling and laughing.

Both of them busted out laughing mostly out of relief.

The screen door was put back up with a sliding bolt on the inside later that day.

CHAPTER THIRTY-EIGHT

FALL, WITH ITS WIND AND SUNNY DAYS, turned suddenly into November and winter arrived with a vengeance.

Both Geraldine and Ray knew the drinking would come back, just not certain when. Ray had been very edgy and cross. Geraldine had more or less quit asking him anything as he snapped at her no matter what the question was.

The only middle ground was Marjory which was still the centerpiece and the reason they where still together. Geraldine had no place else to go, she hadn't even considered it. Marjory was coming up to being a year old and she was a delight. She could say da da and ma ma and milk. She made them both laugh and that was a rarity anymore in the household.

Ray decided in late November that they needed to go to town to get Marjory a birthday present. Geraldine agreed as she needed to get some ingredients to make a cake for the little ones birthday.

Geraldine was very anxious about Rays drinking and

wondered what the trip would bring.

They rode to town in silence with a certain amount of dread on Geraldine's part.

Ray dropped her off at the store with a request for her to get Marjory something nice.

He headed straight for the pool hall and a drink was before him even as he sat down.

He'd made up his mind to go after a couple and managed to do so, with some effort. He ordered a bottle to go with him and hid it in the buggy.

He went back to the store and picked Geraldine and Marjory up and headed for home. Geraldine noticed a distinct personality change right away and she could smell the whiskey. He was much more talkative on the way home and laughed and joked.

She thought if only he could just stay in this mood when he drank, but she knew better.

CHAPTER THIRTY-NINE

MARJORY'S BIRTHDAY CAME AND WENT. She as most one year olds wasn't really aware of anything except maybe a little more attention. Not that she lacked any since she was the glue that kept the two adults together.

Ray was now drinking every day and kept his bottle in the barn. When he ran out he went to town or to the bootlegger Joe Kreitz who was 10 miles to the northeast.

A dark cloud settled over the household. There was no hope of Ray sobering up and both knew it.

December 11th started out as any other day and Ray promptly picked a fight with Geraldine over something stupid to make his excuse for heading to town. He said something on the order of ,"I can't live with someone who picks at me all the time, and I'm going to town." Geraldine hadn't said anything but. "Have you eaten anything this morning?"

Marjory had started to cry because of the arguing and when he stomped off in the snow towards the barn she was crying da da.

He saddled ol' Bouncer and Geraldine watched as he rode southeast toward town with tears in her eyes.

CHAPTER FORTY

RAY HAD BEEN DRUNK FOR TWO DAYS when the blizzard hit on Friday afternoon. From his perch on the bar stool he couldn't see across the street to the grain elevator, let alone the railroad tracks further to the north. It was snowing hard and the wind howled at 30 to 40 miles per hour. Drifting was already bad, and with this amount of snow it really shut everything down. If Ray had thought about heading for home it was too late now.

Geraldine was beside herself. Ray had been gone two full days and the firewood was low as well as the food supplies. Her biggest concern was the stove and keeping the fire going. The supply of matches was down to two. As she went to bed on Friday night she built the fire up and planned to get up in the night to keep it going without wasting her two matches. She hadn't really slept very well for the last two nights so she was exhausted. The blizzard howled outside trying to creep into the cracks around the door and windows. Geraldine finally slept the sleep of the dead.

She awoke at 7 am scared as hell because she hadn't stirred in the night and the fire was out!

CHAPTER FORTY-ONE

GERALDINE LEAPED OUT OF BED and as fast as she could she had to build a fire. It was bitter cold and the wind was still howling outside. Inside the old homestead shack it wasn't much warmer as it leaked everywhere.

She carefully placed her kindling, paper and her smaller wood into the stove and with a small prayer lit the first match. It spurted and died. God help me Geraldine said out loud. She used the last match and it lit the torn up paper and the kindling. Soon the shack was starting to warm up, but Geraldine was scared and shaky thinking about what could have been. The cold was creeping into her being. She was afraid very afraid. She had used the last match! What would happen to her and her baby girl if she allowed herself to let the fire go out again. She gazed at the sleeping one year old and shuddered.

Ray awoke in his own puke and pushed his way out of bed in the back room of the pool hall where he slept the past couple of nights. His head hurt and he could smell himself, the sweat and puke and the stale whiskey. He knew he needed to go home, but after he washed up and looked outside he knew that was impossible. Old man winter was heaving snow and wind at Northern Montana with a vengeance.

CHAPTER FORTY-TWO

BY NOON SHE HAD MADE UP HER MIND. She had only enough firewood and a little coal for two more days, today and tomorrow. Her matches were gone and she didn't know if she could stay awake to keep the fire going.

She was going to take Marjory and try to walk to Lucy's a mile and a half away.

She reasoned if she could make it that far she would be safe and warm. She needed help in the worst way and she was scared to death.

She wrote a short note and left it on the table. "I'm scared and am taking Marjory to Lucy's."

Geraldine had a helluva time getting the old door to the shack open. It had leaked so much air that it was frozen shut. The warm air inside had iced the cracks shut. She had to pour the water from the tea kettle on the stove along the cracks of the door to get it open. There was a drift the size of a Shetland pony right outside the door.

She had bundled herself and Marjory up as well as she

could and making her way out the door over the snow drift had her sweating with the effort.

The wind had let up a little and she thought all she had to do was to make her way to Cottonwood Crick a quarter of a mile away. Then follow it down for about a mile and a quarter to Lucy's where there was warmth and safety.

CHAPTER FORTY-THREE

RAY WAS FAIRLY SOBER BY NOON and the wind had let up a little. He had about three whiskeys to steady his shakes. The first one had come up almost instantly, but the last two steadied him somewhat.

He got ol' Bouncer out of the livery stable and started home. He was ashamed and scared when he remembered how little wood and coal there was and he hoped Geraldine knew where he kept the extra matches in the barn.

He wasn't five miles out of town when the wind had come up again with a vengeance. He and ol' Bouncer couldn't see a thing. He knew he was close to Missus Wolfe's place, but he couldn't be sure. The *white out* that was the blizzard made it impossible to see. Even though he had traveled this way drunk and sober a thousand times, the *white out* made him disoriented.

Suddenly the old horse stumbled and Ray was thrown violently into the snow hitting hard. It took a few moments for him to gather himself because he had hit so hard. Ray was grateful for the snow as it broke some of his fall.

Ol' Bouncer wasn't as lucky. He had stepped into a badger hole hidden in the snow. His front leg was broken and he whinnied in pain.

"Oh God Damn it all to Hell," Ray said when he could see what was going on. He knew what had to be done, Bouncer couldn't go any more. The only other choice was to let his old friend freeze to death with his pain.

Broken legs on horses couldn't be fixed and Ray knew this. He comforted Bouncer with his left hand and with tears in his eyes freezing because of the wind he raised his old Colt Revolver. Goodbye my old friend. The shot was muffled in the wind and hid Ray's crying. He and the old horse had gone a lot of miles together. Now that was over and his friend was gone.

Ray knew he'd be gone if he couldn't find his way to Missus Wolfe's pretty damn quick. He was freezing already.

CHAPTER FORTY-FOUR

GERALDINE HAD FOUND HER WAY to the crick and was struggling along carrying her precious cargo. Marjory was whimpering and Geraldine was already exhausted. The wind had really started to blow hard again and Geraldine had an awful time even seeing the cottonwood trees that lined the crick. The drifting and the blowing snow made it more difficult to walk because you couldn't ever be sure of where you were stepping. She fell down numerous times always managing to hang onto the one year old baby.

She was getting very, very cold in spite of her working so hard. Her legs felt like lead and they were getting numb. Her fingers were numb and her face hurt from the cold and the wind. She knew it was below zero and the wind made it feel worse.

She finally had to sit down on a boulder which stuck out of the snow near a tree. She rocked her baby trying to comfort her. The wind drowned out her voice and the baby wouldn't be comforted.

"Oh God," Geraldine cried, "Please help us." She knew if they didn't reach Lucy's soon that they would be in trouble.

Up she got again and struggled on toward safety. She fell again and lost her grip on Marjory. Scrambling up she grabbed her baby and walked some more. She had no idea how far she had gone or how far it was to Lucy's as the *white out* blizzard made everything look the same.

The more she struggled forward the more exhausted she became. Surprisingly she was getting warm. She didn't understand it, but she was getting very warm. This feels good she thought. The baby was now quiet and very heavy or so it seemed.

She stopped again under a tree and sat down in the snow with her back against the tree. She was too warm and needed to lay the baby down to take off some of the hot clothes.

She lay the quiet baby down and struggled to get her coat off. She put it down and set the baby on the coat and wrapped her up.

Lord she was tired, she would close her eyes for just a moment then go on.

"Thank you Lord for warming me up," she said and closed her eyes to rest.

CHAPTER FORTY-FIVE

RAY KNEW HE HAD TO BE CLOSE to the widow Wolfe's homestead. He had struck out in what he thought and hoped was an easterly direction toward her shack. He knew if he didn't get there pretty quick he and ol' Bouncer would be found after the storm let up, both dead.

He didn't know how far he had gone when suddenly the wind let up for just a moment and he spotted the shack a little to the east and south of him. "Thank God," Ray said out loud as he knew he would have missed it if the wind hadn't let up just that little bit.

He struggled toward his goal and the wind and snow engulfed the tiny shack again.

Finally he made the door and beat on it repeatedly to make himself heard above the wind and howling storm.

The widow Wolfe came loaded for bear with her old double barrel 20 gauge shotgun to the door. After yelling out, "Who is there," and after Ray answered, they both worked on the door for a few minutes to get it open.

Missus Wolfe was a sawed off little woman who was almost as wide as she was tall. She smoked roll your own Bull Durham and had permanent nicotine stains on her hands. She swore enough to make a sailor blush, but as hard as she was on the outside, it hid the tenderhearted person she was. She worked the land by herself and could hold her own with any of the homesteaders.

It was close to an hour before Ray thawed out by the old cook stove. He knew he was lucky as hell, but the more he sobered up and thought about his girls the more worried he became. Surely Geraldine would not be foolish enough to go someplace in a blizzard.

Ray and Missus Wolfe convinced each other that Geraldine would certainly stay close to home and both she and Marjory would be fine. When the storm let up, Ray would head out again with a borrowed horse from Missus Wolfe.

Ray tried to sleep but it came in starts and fits. He couldn't really rest as he was constantly thinking about his girls. Exhausted he finally did sleep, only to dream about the blizzard, ol' Bouncer, and his girls.

CHAPTER FORTY-SIX

SUNDAY MORNING THE SKY WAS A BRILLIANT BLUE and the wind had stopped. The scene was all white. It made you blink your eyes. With the sun reflecting off the all white terrain it was almost blinding outside.

Ray saddled Missus Wolfe's old mare and thanking her, he made for home. He didn't stay for breakfast but took her up on an offer of biscuits to take home.

It was slow going, because of the deep and drifted snow. The old mare had to pick her way around the deepest drifts.

Ray didn't stop anywhere, because he had a feeling of foreboding as he rode. He wrote it off as a feeling of guilt about being drunk for days.

It took a good two hours to go from Missus Wolfe's to the shack. He hurried the last half mile on account of he couldn't see any smoke coming from the chimney. "Oh God," he said out loud, "let them be alright."

His heart dropped as he piled off the horse and ran to the house. The door had blown open from the storm and there was a drift in the house. He searched the house and then the barn running like a mad man calling their names.

The more he searched the worse he felt. While he was in the barn he looked on the shelf where he kept the extra matches, they were still there, two full boxes.

He searched the house again and then the yard for tracks. Of course there were none, the wind had gobbled up any trace.

The note Geraldine had left had blown off the table and was in the drifted snow by the door, Ray never saw it. If he had he wouldn't have felt any better.

After another round through the house and barn and the yard he caught the old mare. Ray started for Frank and Lucy Soldier's place a mile and a half away.

CHAPTER FORTY-SEVEN

FRANK SOLDIER PUSHED THE DOOR OPEN and blinked a couple of times, he shaded his eyes from the brilliance of the beautiful white landscape. The blizzard had blown itself out and you could hear every footstep in the snowdrifts as he went out toward the barn. His old dog had been housebound for days and was just as happy as Frank to be outside.

As he was picking his way to the barn to check on the livestock something caught his eye over by the crick. It was something blue that was out of place in a sea of white. He stared at the blue then started toward it. When he was about 30 feet away he yelled out loud, "Oh my God."

There was Geraldine sitting with her back against a cottonwood tree frozen stiff without her coat. Frank quickly looked around and suddenly his gaze was drawn to a small drift beside Geraldine. He ran over and brushed the snow away. Little Marjory's body lay under the snow drift still wrapped in the old wool coat. "OH NO, OH NO,

OH NO, OH GOD NO," he yelled into the stillness of the white landscape.

Geraldine and Marjory were only 75 yards from the house. Only 75 yards to safety.

CHAPTER FORTY-EIGHT

WHEN RAY CAME RIDING THE OLD MARE toward the Soldier's house, Lucy was with Frank by the crick next to the bodies. Lucy was weeping and wringing her hands. Ray slid off the horse and ran the last 20 yards. He dropped to his knees beside the bodies and buried his face in his hands. He sobbed like a small child. "My fault, my fault," he kept sobbing.

All three of them stayed this way for 10 or 15 minutes, each with their own misery and thoughts.

Finally, Frank told Lucy to check on their kids. He gently told Ray they needed to get the sled and move Geraldine and Marjory to the barn.

When Frank got the sled he and Ray lifted Geraldine on to it. Then Ray carefully picked up his precious Marjory and, sobbing uncontrollably, laid her beside her mother on the sled.

They laid them in the old barn on some fresh hay and covered them with a blanket.

Frank said he would ride to town to contact the authorities. Ray didn't say a word, he just sat next to the bodies and sobbed.

CHAPTER FORTY-NINE

THE FUNERAL TO RAY WAS SOMETHING that felt unreal. The service was held in Dayton at the white Baptist Church on the hill. Ray heard nothing the preacher said, he only looked down at his hands and cried. The coffin was large enough for both mother and child and the church was packed.

Afterwards a reception was held in the basement of the church. Everyone attended. Ray was in a fog and all the condolences were wasted on him. He kept repeating to himself that it was his fault.

The casket was closed and Ray had decided to bury them in the cemetery at Bull Hook Bottoms 30 miles to the east where they had married.

He rode the train to the Bottoms with the casket. He rented a cheap room at the Fair Hotel and promptly got drunk.

The next morning he went to the cemetery to observe the burying. The frozen earth had been chipped away for a half a day by two men using a pick and shovel.

When the casket containing both bodies was lowered

into the frozen earth Ray's heart split in two. He broke down and cried again.

He had no money for a marker; the last of his money had gone for the funeral, casket, train ride, hotel room, and rot-gut whiskey.

As he stood there crying he asked God to take him too, his life was over. All that was precious to him was now being covered up by frozen clods of dirt and he didn't want to live.

CHAPTER FIFTY

CHRISTMAS CAME AND WENT IN THAT WINTER of 1928/29. Ray hadn't drawn a sober breath since the funeral. He sold what little possessions he had to keep drinking and by spring he had nothing left to sell except his homestead shack and his land.

He looked like hell and felt worse. Ray hadn't bathed or shaved and had eaten very little. He looked like death. He hadn't been home for a month or so. He just passed out in the back room of the pool hall when he had drank enough that particular day.

Whenever anyone said anything to him he just said, "My life is over and my beautiful daughter and my wife are in the ground." Then he would start his litany of "It's my fault." People avoided him like the plague. There was no sense in talking to him. He was in the depths of depression and was hell bent on trying to drink himself to death. The thought of suicide came and went, but he knew sooner or later the bottle would get the job done.

Finally, in May of 1929, he was throwing up blood and what little he ate came back up right away. He was bleeding inside; his guts were eating on each other.

Red, the barkeep, finally talked old man Wasford into hauling Ray into Bull Hook Bottoms to the hospital before he died in the pool hall. Red wasn't so much concerned with Ray as he knew a dead body in the back room was messy to clean up and bad for business.

Ray was too weak to protest so he ended up in the hospital not really expecting to live. He had lost 25 to 30 pounds and looked 75 years old.

About midnight of the first day he went into the delirium tremors or as it's affectionately known to drunks as the DT's, the shakes, or the snakes. Take your pick of descriptions it's all the same thing.

For three days and nights he yelled and screamed for a drink as the black panther was sitting on his chest. He was bothered by the little mouse carrying a bale of hay on his back which kept coming out of the wall.

Ol' Doc Jesture had no sympathy for drunks. He told the nurses to just strap Ray down and if he lived he lived.

Some of the nurses were kind enough to slip him a small drink of whiskey or he would have been dead for sure. He wanted to die, but like all of us when faced with the reality of it, he was afraid. Finally the worst of it started to subside.

CHAPTER FIFTY-ONE

AFTER FIVE DAYS THEY PUT RAY INTO A ROOM with another man. Ray was finally able to eat something and hold it down. The old doc had showed up and said basically you are going to die if you continue to drink. He added that he was surprised that Ray had lived through this last bout. Without another word he turned and left.

For the next two days Ray didn't say a helluva lot, he just stared at the wall.

Finally he felt the urge to talk and the only audience he had was his roommate. All Ray's troubles came out and his explanation for his drinking. Ray thought he made a good case and believed anyone listening to such a good argument would tell him that it was fine to drink himself to death.

Al Forester was a quiet, religious man and very polite. He listened to Ray's litany for about an hour in silence. Finally he said, "Yes, I know how you feel. My wife died last year in child birth. My child died too. I'm in here diagnosed with cancer. The difference between me and you is I want to live. I'm not trying to kill myself with the drink. I know all things happen for a reason and I'm not going to feel sorry for myself like you. I know that life is a gift from the good Lord. You ought to be ashamed of yourself trying to throw your life away by feeling sorry for yourself."

There followed a silence that was very loud in its own way.

Neither man knew what to say, so nothing was said the rest of the afternoon.

CHAPTER FIFTY-TWO

RAY WAS WEAK AND PEAKED LOOKING when they turned him out of the hospital. He grunted his goodbye to Al and muttered he hoped he would get better.

Ray hitched a ride to Dayton with the delivery truck for the lumber yard.

He borrowed a horse and headed for home which he hadn't seen in a month and a half. It was in shambles, he'd done nothing since Geraldine and little Marjory had died.

He only swept the place out and got on the horse again and headed for Frank and Lucy Soldier's place.

He hadn't seen either of them since the funeral. When he got near the ranch the first thing he saw was the Soldier's two little ones playing in the yard.

He wiped the tears from his eyes and greeted the wee ones. Their folks came out of the house and barn and waved hello.

He stayed the afternoon and into the evening enjoying their company. Ray especially enjoyed their little girl

Molly. She was a delight. Ray had a hard time not crying, but made his mind up he wouldn't for all their sakes.

As the day progressed he had an idea. He presented it to Frank and Lucy. Ray would let them share/crop his homestead and they would put the crop in. They would get 4/5 of the crop and Ray would get 1/5. He told them he just couldn't stay on the place as everywhere he looked he was reminded of his girls. Ray said he needed a new start. He left with a hand shake on the deal and hugged the kids.

As he rode the mile and a half northwest he continued wiping the tears from his eyes.

CHAPTER FIFTY-THREE

RAY HAD FINALLY WRITTEN HIS MOTHER in Kansas after he left the hospital. He told her of his marriage and the birth of his baby girl. He finished up by telling her the rest of the story. She, in a return letter, had suggested they take a trip to Oregon to see Ray's aunt Lil, which was his ma's only sister. She said maybe it would help Ray to get away for awhile.

Ray's step-dad had passed away and his mother had a little money saved up. She made her way to Bull Hook Bottoms from Kansas and Ray met her there. They boarded the Great Northern passenger train and headed west.

Ray had stayed sober the past month by sheer will and had kept himself away from town. He cleaned and discarded things at the house. There wasn't much sleep as the memories haunted him. He walked the prairie at night a lot.

The trip to Oregon was pleasant and he was glad to have his mother there to talk to. They had never been close. Sometimes a tragedy helps the situation. They were able to talk for the first time in their lives, really talk. Ray poured out his pain and hurt and guilt and his ma listened. She in turn told him about her regrets in life and how she had turned to God to help her. He listened really, but kept saying on the inside, I know it's my fault my girls are gone.

They visited Ray's aunt for about a week. Ray's mother had decided to go back to Kansas. Ray thought he'd cross over to Washington State and maybe look up some of Geraldine's kin before making his way back to Montana.

The day of departure started early for the two as they prepared for their respective journeys. They made their way to the train station with plenty of time to catch his mom's train.

Ray felt a closeness to his mother he had never felt before. They had shared together and both felt like they knew the other better and a new bond had been formed. It's good to have family Ray had said to her this morning and to his aunt.

He was really sorry to see her go. Not wanting to cry he walked up and down the platform to kill some time and keep his mind off of her leaving.

Ray felt a little guilty about borrowing some money from his mom, but he knew as soon as he got home he would send her what he borrowed and more. He had decided to go back to work doing something with his time instead of thinking all the time about his girls. He thought maybe he would go to work in town for someone instead of isolating himself on the homestead.

He decided he'd buy a paper for his mom to read on her ride toward home. He made his way inside the depot to get one.

CHAPTER FIFTY-FOUR

WHEN RAY STEPPED BACK ON THE PLATFORM the train had just stopped and people were screaming, "She fell, she fell, oh God, oh God." Ray couldn't really see what was going on as a cluster of people blocked him from the train and whatever had occurred.

He searched the crowd for his mother and couldn't immediately find her face. Suddenly he got a terrible feeling. He rushed to the throng of people and pushed his way through to the edge of the tracks on the raised platform. Looking down he nearly passed out as he saw his mother's old shoes and part of her dress.

Ma, Ma he shouted as he jumped down between the train and the platform. He heard someone yelling at the top of their lungs, a hurt animal cry. He realized it was he that was yelling. He couldn't really take it all in. In front of him was the mangled body of what had been his mother. The mother that he had just gotten to know.

Someone pulled him up from his knees and helped him

from between the platform and the tracks.

All that followed seemed like it was happening in a dream. Ray couldn't focus, he was numb.

He kept running it over and over in his mind. What happened, what could I have done? What could I have done? No answers came, none.

CHAPTER FIFTY-FIVE

RAY DRANK HIS WAY FROM OREGON TO WASHINGTON, across Idaho and back to Montana. He drank to kill the pain of thinking and living. All he loved was gone and he couldn't bear to think about it.

He came back to Dayton sometime that summer and holed up in the pool hall and proceeded to try to drink himself to death.

Ray woke on an extremely hot morning in August to a pounding head, dry mouth and guts trying to eat each other.

He wasn't aware of much that morning except a terrible smell. He realized, after a couple of groggy minutes, the smell was him. He was full of self-loathing when it came to him he had crapped himself. Ray knew that this was the only clothes he had. His self disgust was worse than ever. He was overwhelmed by it all. Ray whispered out loud, "God help me, please!"

He crawled to the door and out of the pool hall to the back where he started to puke and shake. He repeated it again, "God please help me!"

Ray cleaned himself up as well as he could with water from the hand pump outside the pool hall. He made it to the outside privy and stripped down. He cut away his old nasty underwear with a knife and threw them down the privy's hole.

He dressed again and made his way inside where he borrowed some clothes from Red, the barkeep.

Although shaking badly he didn't take a drink that morning. By the afternoon he felt good enough that he decided to go across the street to the post office to get his mail. He hadn't even touched his mail in a couple of weeks.

He had a time trying to open the combination mail box with the shakes, luckily the city's old ladies had come and gone so there was no audience to the tremors.

Ray had a bunch of ordinary letters, which consisted mainly of bills. One letter stood out from the rest however. He went outside and sat on the bench facing east toward the pool hall and opened it.

CHAPTER FIFTY-SIX

RAY QUICKLY TURNED THE LETTER OVER and saw it was signed Al Forester, his roommate in the hospital at Bull Hook Bottoms. Something else was in the envelope, he dug it out. It was Al Forester's obituary from the newspaper in Bull Hook Bottoms. He had died of his cancer last week at the age of 46.

Ray had a pounding head and a raw gut and none of this was making a lot of sense right now. He turned the letter over again and a small note with different handwriting caught his eye. The note was in the margin of the letter and said, I found this beside Mr. Forester's bedside table, sending on to you Mr. Frost, along with his obituary. It was signed Amy Whitehouse, Nurse.

Ray tried to focus his eyes on the note. Finally squinting he read the letter.

Ray,

By the time you get this I will be dead. Thought

I'd try one more time to get through your thick skull.

I read in the paper that your mother had died and how it occurred. There is no doubt in my mind you now have fallen back into the "I'm gonna drink because I have a right to thinking." I hope you read this before you die drunk.

I want you to know I would trade you in a minute, because although you do have an immense amount of pain and misery, all you have to do is stop drinking and you will live. You see I want to live more than anything, but I don't have that choice anymore.

Remember when I said to you all things happen for a reason. Maybe my dying will be for a reason if you stop and think for one moment that you still have your life. Please don't throw it away.

Ray do you think your loving wife and your beautiful daughter and your mother would want you to throw your life away? There may be someone who needs your help. Quit feeling sorry for yourself and start living.

On my death bed, I ask you to at least consider what I'm saying.

Your friend,
Al Forester

P.S. The Good Lord forgives you, Ray Frost. You are not God, and only God can judge us. When we judge ourselves we are playing God. Remember Ray you are not God.

All Ray could do was weep. He couldn't stop. The whole thing looked crystal clear. Damn that little man, but he was right. What had possessed him to write me on his death bed. All he could do was cry and cry and shake some more.

CHAPTER FIFTY-SEVEN

IT WAS SIX WEEKS LATER and Ray was still walking the streets of Dayton most nights, but he was still sober. Something had changed, he couldn't put his finger on it, but he knew he wanted to live more than he wanted to die. Some days he only hung on by a thread, but he was still sober.

This beautiful fall morning he had walked until 3 A.M., then fell into a fitful sleep until 6 and now was walking again.

It was Sunday morning and people were stirring to go to services or just getting moving.

Ray had walked about two hours and was deep in his own thoughts. He had his head down and wasn't paying attention when he almost bumped into a little five or six year old girl. She was obviously on her way to Sunday school at the little white church on the hill. She had her little brother in tow.

She was a very pretty little girl with her Sunday best yellow dress and a yellow ribbon in her hair. She gave Ray a beautiful smile and said that her name was Emma and her brother was Ralphie.

Ray introduced himself and shook their hands. Emma said, "Oh I know who you are Mr. Frost. My mamma said you had a little girl like me and she froze to death. She says you hurt real bad inside cause she's gone. I'm so sorry for you."

She reached out her hand again and said, "I'm going to God's House maybe he can help. You want to walk with Ralphie and me?"

Ray's eyes teared up and he took her hand.

THE END.